VLAD
THE WORLD'S
WORST
VAMPIRE

For Aggy – who helped me with vampire names!
– A.W.

For Mat̶̶̶̶̶̶̶̶̶̶̶̶̶̶̶̶̶̶̶̶̶̶̶̶̶̶̶̶̶̶̶̶̶̶̶̶̶ocolates

STRIPES PUBLISHING
An imprint of the Little Tiger Group
1 Coda Studios, 189 Munster Road,
London SW6 6AW

A paperback original
First published in Great Britain in 2018

Text copyright © Anna Wilson, 2018
Illustrations copyright © Kathryn Durst, 2018

ISBN: 978-1-84715-914-4

VLAD

THE WORLD'S
WORST
VAMPIRE

Fang-tastic Friends

ANNA WILSON

ILLUSTRATED BY
KATHRYN DURST

Stripes

1

Vlad had been working on his vampire skills since dusk on Friday, under the strict guidance of his mother, Mortemia. Now it was Sunday night and Vlad had still not managed to do anything to please her – as usual. Finally, with a howl of frustration, his mother had shouted at him to "get out of my sight" and had stormed off to her room.

That had been hours ago and now it was nearly midnight and Mortemia still hadn't reappeared. Vlad's pet bat Flit was trying to

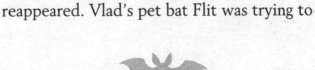

distract him from his worries.

"Let's play hide-and-seek," he squeaked. "I'll hide!"

"No! I'm too nervous," Vlad protested. He was in the corridor outside his parents' room, trying to listen in to their conversation, but he couldn't make out what they were saying behind the heavy oak door.

"I'm sure they're talking about me," Vlad went on. Then he realized Flit was no longer listening – the little bat had flown away to hide.

"Where are you, Flit?" Vlad whispered. He crept along the corridor, peering anxiously into dark corners.

He was soon so worried about trying to find Flit in the scary shadows that he almost forgot about his parents. He hunted high and low, shuddering whenever he touched a spider's web and wheezing as he looked under cushions that sent up a cloud of dust when he moved them. He took a puff of his inhaler before carrying on his search.

"Flit?" he repeated. "Where are you?"

At last, peeking in between a large oak chest and a suit of armour, he spotted the bat.

"Found you!" Vlad cried.

"Impressive," said Flit, coming out of his

7

hiding place. "I think your night vision must be getting better. It was pretty dark down there." He shook himself free of cobwebs.

The little vampire grinned, showing his tiny fangs. "Playing hide-and-seek indoors isn't as scary as I thought it would be," he said. "Apart from the spiders… Do you think I might finally get over my fear of the dark?"

Flit performed a gleeful loop-the-loop. "Of course! We'll soon have you racing about the graveyard at night."

Vlad was about to protest when the door to his parents' bedroom creaked open and his father, Count Drax Impaler, came out.

"What nonsense are you and that bat up to now?" he asked, looking stern.

Vlad looked at the floor. "Nothing, Father," he said.

Count Drax pursed his blood-red lips.

"Hmmm. Well, as it happens, I was on my way to find you. Your mother and I have something we want to tell you. Come in here."

Vlad bit his lip as he felt all his anxiety return. "Umm, OK," he said.

"Don't worry," Flit whispered in his ear. "I'll be with you—"

But Drax had whisked Vlad into the room and shut the door before the little bat could follow.

"Rude!" Flit squeaked from behind the door.

The little vampire followed his father into the vast, icy-cold bedroom. His parents slept in a four-poster double coffin with a deep red canopy over it. His mother was sitting on the edge of the coffin now. To Vlad's surprise, Grandpa Gory was also in the room, fast asleep in one of the carved wooden armchairs by the wardrobe. He let out an enormous, loud snore.

Mortemia rolled her eyes. "We should never have tried to include *him* in our discussions, Drax," she said, nodding at Gory. Then to Vlad she said, "Come and sit down, my little devil." She patted the bedspread. "We've been discussing your progress."

"Oh," said Vlad. His shoulders fell.

This is definitely not going to be good news, he thought.

"As you know," Mortemia continued, "our last session on mastering mind control was a spectacular failure. If you can't make one little object move, how will you ever learn to persuade other creatures to do things against their will? Mind control is a simple skill, which vampires have had for centuries. I can't understand what you find so difficult about it."

She was right: Vlad had been unable to make anything happen by the power of his mind. He just found it so hard to concentrate on things like making a glass of blood move along the dining table or persuading the spiders to tidy away their webs. He would start off thinking hard but then his mind would wander and he would begin to feel sleepy. He was feeling pretty sleepy right now, in fact.

He yawned and his mother immediately

told him off. "Cover your mouth! It's extremely rude to show your fangs, Vlad."

"Sorry, Mother," Vlad muttered. "But that mind-control stuff is exhausting. I've been trying to do it all weekend."

"And you'll be doing it all next week, too, at this rate," Mortemia said.

Vlad groaned. He really wanted to go to his room now and get a couple of hours' sleep before dawn. Tomorrow was Monday and he was planning on going to human school again. He couldn't wait to see his best friend Minxie and his teacher Miss Lemondrop, but going to school in the day *and* having lessons with Mother at night was wearing him out.

Drax coughed loudly and Vlad snapped to attention as he realized Mortemia was still speaking.

"…which is why we've decided you need to spend some time with other vampires,"

she finished.

Vlad was puzzled. "But you've always said that there *are* no other vampires."

"Not around *here*, no," said Drax slowly.

Vlad's pale face went from white to green. "No! You don't mean...?"

"Yes, you're going to Transylvania," said his mother.

"But I don't want to," Vlad exclaimed. "I'm happy here!"

Drax laughed. "Mwhahaha. We don't mean for *ever*."

"Although that *is* an idea," said Mortemia with a sniff.

"No!" Vlad cried, beginning to panic. If he just disappeared, what would Minxie think? How would he get a note to Miss Lemondrop to explain why he was absent? His chest began to heave and he struggled to catch his breath. He reached inside his cape for his inhaler and took a long hard puff.

Grandpa Gory woke up suddenly.

"What's that?" he barked, blinking in confusion. He noticed poor Vlad was wheezing and went to pat him on the back.

"What have you said to the little devil now?" he asked Mortemia.

"You can stay out of this, Gory," snapped Mortemia. "Why don't you go back to sleep? *Without* the snoring, thank you," she added.

"When everyone has finished arguing," Drax said, "perhaps you'll allow me to explain, Vladimir. A couple of months with your cousin Lupus will make you see how to become a truly bad little vampire." Drax rubbed his long thin hands together. "Lupus is an *excellent* example of evilness. You should hear his laugh – it's so terrifying, he managed to break a whole chandelier!"

"If only you could laugh like that, Vlad," Mortemia said wistfully.

"But I can!" cried Vlad. "Listen." He threw back his head and gave an evil laugh. "MwhahaheeheehhhhhAARGH—!" But he was still rather wheezy and he collapsed into another coughing fit.

"Useless," Mortemia said, shaking her head.

"I *can* do it sometimes," he spluttered.

"Sometimes isn't enough!" Drax roared.

"You need to ALWAYS laugh like a proper vampire, just as you need to ALWAYS be able to use mind control and ALWAYS be able to finish drinking your glass of blood without complaining!"

"I'll get better at those things as I get older," said Vlad. He was feeling anxious. He'd never met his cousin but he'd heard plenty about him. "You thought I'd never learn how to turn into a bat but I can now. Look!" He squeezed his eyes shut and thought, *Batwings – Air – Travel* and POOF! he was a bat, whizzing above his parents, turning loop-the-loops and squeaking in bat language, "Can I get my Bat Licence soon?"

"Yes, yes," Drax said, swatting at the air irritably. "Don't change the subject. Your bat-morphing is hardly impressive. You still won't join me on an outdoor night-flight."

Vlad landed back down in vampire form

with a thump. "I don't want to go to Transylvania," he said sulkily.

"Mulch is already packing your things," said Mortemia. "You're going tonight."

Vlad gasped. He needed to think of something to put them off this plan – and quickly.

If only Flit weren't locked outside, I could ask him for an idea, he thought.

"Run along now," his mother said. "There's no time to lose."

"I can't go," Vlad blurted out. "I-it's dangerous for me to fly long distances when I've had an asthma attack," he said.

Mortemia snorted. "Ridiculous—" she started.

"That's true," Grandpa Gory interrupted. "Remember what Dr Freakenstein said the last time you wrote to him about Vlad's condition? He was quite clear that Vlad

should wait at least twenty-four hours after the end of an attack before attempting a long-distance flight."

"Very helpful, Gory," Mortemia muttered sarcastically.

Vlad shot his grandfather a grateful look. "He also said that new places could make my asthma worse," he said. This was a fib, but Vlad was desperate.

Drax frowned. "I don't remember that part."

Luckily Gory was very much on Vlad's side. "Ah, yes. New environments could be dangerous – I remember that. Perhaps you and Mortemia should go to Transylvania first, to make sure everything will be all right for Vlad's stay?" he suggested. "You know – check the bedcovers are feather-free and so on?" he added.

"I really don't think that'll be necessary,"

said Mortemia.

"Oh, I don't know," said Drax. "I think it's a good idea. We could discuss plans in more depth with Pavlova and Maximus, perhaps?"

"No, this is … idiotic!" Mortemia cried. "We've already come up with a plan – I don't see why you should listen to that old fool," she added, glowering at Gory.

Grandpa Gory raised his eyebrows knowingly and Vlad tried not to smile. Mortemia never wanted to go to Transylvania. She hated Drax's sister, Aunt Pavlova, and disapproved of the modern style in which she lived.

"But Mortemia, we *could* make it into a romantic mini-break," Drax drawled. He took his wife's hand in his. "We could see that musical you've been talking about. You know – *Bats*?"

Mortemia's eyes lit up but she said nothing.

"Ah, *Bats*!" said Grandpa Gory. "What a show!"

"Exactly – *everyone* has seen it in Transylvania." Drax's voice became smoother and more persuasive. "What's more, Mortemia, I could take you to your favourite store, Bloodingdales? I'll buy you a new cape for the theatre. You would be the most delightful-looking vampire there," he added.

"I *do* need a new cape," Mortemia said, her frown melting. "I could do with a new pair of boots, too. Oh, you've won me over, my darling devil. I'll go and pack right now!"

Drax kissed Mortemia's hand. "My wicked one! We'll leave before dawn. This will be the trip of a lifetime, my rotten little worm!"

Vlad turned away and pulled a face. He hated it when his parents got all soppy in front of him. He did feel relieved, however – he had managed to get out of the trip.

For the time being, at least.

Drax and Mortemia left later that night – but not before they had given Vlad a list of tasks to complete by their return:

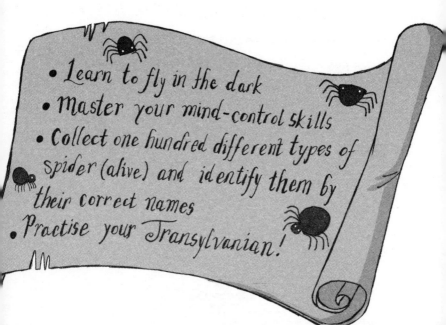

- Learn to fly in the dark
- Master your mind-control skills
- Collect one hundred different types of spider (alive) and identify them by their correct names
- Practise your Transylvanian!

Vlad had gulped when he'd read it.

"When will you be back?" he'd asked, hoping it would be long enough for them to have forgotten about the list.

His parents had both answered at once:

"I shouldn't think it will take more than a couple of days," Mortemia had said.

At the very same time, Drax had said, "I think we'll need a couple of weeks to take in all the sights and sort things out with Lupus."

"TWO WEEKS with your family?"

"Yes," said Drax firmly. "We'll be back in two weeks. That should leave Vlad plenty of time to carry out all his tasks to perfection, don't you think?"

This last comment had convinced Vlad's mother.

"Very well," she had said. "See you in a fortnight, Vlad – and you had better make sure you've done *everything* by then!"

After saying goodbye, Vlad went to his
room in the East Wing. He pushed open the
oak door and dragged himself to his coffin.
Without even bothering to undress, he closed
his eyes and flopped back on to his bedspread
with a groan, letting the list drop to the floor.

Flit landed next to Vlad. "They've gone –
great!" he squeaked. "Now your parents are
away, you're FREE!" he cried, flipping upside
down and grinning.

"I'm not free, Flit – look at that," Vlad
said, pointing at the list.

Flit picked it up in his mouth and lay it on
the coffin. "Hmm," he said. "That's tough.
But they won't be back for ages."

"They'll be back eventually. And Grandpa
Gory and Mulch are still here to keep an
eye on me," Vlad insisted. "In any case, the

minute Mother and Father are home, I'll be sent away to Transylvania all by myself," he added sorrowfully.

Flit hopped next to Vlad. "Do you think I'd stay here without you?" he said.

"You'd come, too?" Vlad said, sitting up. "Really?"

"Of course," said Flit. "We've always done everything together."

"Thank you," said Vlad, resting his head gently against Flit's.

"Now, now, that's enough soppiness," said a voice.

Vlad leaped from his coffin and Flit shot into the air.

"Grandpa!" Vlad cried.

"Who else would it be? I'm in charge now," said Grandpa Gory. "You'll have to do what I say from now on, young vampire."

Vlad felt his heart sink.

Then Grandpa threw back his head and laughed. "Mwhahahaha! Your *face*! I'm only teasing, Vlad. Forget the list for now – there'll be plenty of time for that later," he said. "I have plans… I've been waiting for an opportunity to try out a potion. This one promises to change anyone who drinks it into a dragon. How about that? I found the recipe in one of my great-great-great uncle's books in the library. I'm going to ask Mulch to get the ingredients. What do you say?"

Vlad didn't want to try a potion that might change him into a dragon. Especially a potion made from ingredients the family butler was in charge of. Cooking was not Mulch's strong point. The only recipes he knew involved blood as their main ingredient.

"The thing is…" Vlad began. But then he realized there was no need for excuses.

Grandpa Gory had already fallen asleep and was snoring loudly.

"Why don't you sleep for a bit, too?" Flit said.

"OK," said Vlad. He yawned. "Wake me up when it's time for school."

"I will," said Flit.

Vlad was having a lovely dream about being in a cookery class at human school. Minxie and he were taking it turns to stir a large bowl of chocolate.

"Mmmm!" Vlad murmured in his sleep. "Smells delicious."

"Thank you," said a voice in his ear.

Vlad sat up with a jolt to find Flit sitting on his coffin, giggling softly.

"Where's Grandpa?" he asked sleepily.

"He went to his own coffin hours ago," said Flit.

"*Hours* ago?" Vlad repeated. He glanced

up at the window and saw that the sun was already shining through a crack in the curtains. "Oh no! What time is it?" he said. "I'm not going to be late, am I?"

"Don't worry," Flit assured him. "I thought I'd leave you to sleep for as long as possible. It's eight o'clock. Look." He pointed to a pocket watch sitting on the side by Vlad's coffin.

Vlad gasped. "But that's Grandpa's!"

"Don't worry. He's always losing it," said Flit. "I thought you'd find it useful. Now, you'd better hurry – you haven't got long. Your uniform is still under the big yew tree in the graveyard where you left it."

"OK. Let's fly then," Vlad said.

Flit shook his head. "I'm not coming with you."

"But we've always done everything together!" said Vlad. "You said so yourself."

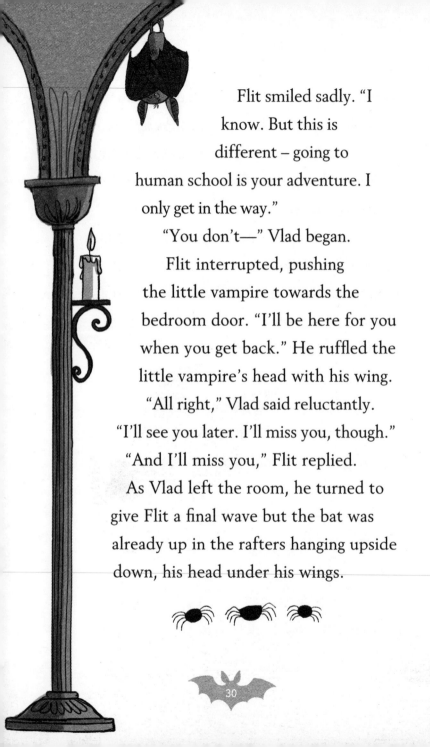

Flit smiled sadly. "I know. But this is different – going to human school is your adventure. I only get in the way."

"You don't—" Vlad began.

Flit interrupted, pushing the little vampire towards the bedroom door. "I'll be here for you when you get back." He ruffled the little vampire's head with his wing.

"All right," Vlad said reluctantly. "I'll see you later. I'll miss you, though."

"And I'll miss you," Flit replied.

As Vlad left the room, he turned to give Flit a final wave but the bat was already up in the rafters hanging upside down, his head under his wings.

Vlad ran to the yew tree and changed into his
school uniform. Then he put his cape back
on so that he could turn into a bat and fly to
school – flying there was so much faster than
walking!

He opened his arms out wide, closed his
eyes and thought *B-A-T*. He transformed
immediately. Then, folding his wings behind
him, he dived down the hill towards the
town.

Children were streaming in through the school gates by the time Vlad arrived. Fortunately they were too busy chattering to notice a small bat whizz over their heads and into the bike shed. This was the safest place for Vlad to change back into vampire form. He kept his cape here, too, because Miss Lemondrop had told him it was not school uniform, so he wasn't allowed to wear it in lessons. He'd also stored his skateboard in the bike shed: he and Minxie sometimes played with it at break time, so if he was caught hanging around the shed, no one would be suspicious.

Minxie was the only one who knew he was a vampire and she was sworn to secrecy. Vlad didn't like to think what might happen if anyone else discovered the truth. His parents always told him that humans hated vampires, although he'd never found out exactly why this was.

Vlad hovered over the bike shed roof, checked none of the children were looking, then zipped inside and thought *Vampire – Land – Air – Down*.

He gave a muffled yelp as he landed in a crumpled heap on the hard floor.

He was picking himself up and dusting himself down when he heard a chuckle and someone said, "Still need some practice, then?"

He recognized the voice at once. "Hello, Minxie!" he said, beaming. "Where did you come from?"

"I was hiding in here, waiting for you!" she said, and threw her arms round him. Then she looked around the shed.

"Where's Flit?"

Vlad's grin faded. "He didn't want to come. He said this was my adventure. I hope I haven't upset him."

"Maybe he wanted a snooze," said Minxie.

Vlad remembered the little bat hanging upside down. "Yes, probably," he said.

"Anyway, I missed you over the weekend," Minxie said. "Did you have fun?"

"No, it was boring," said Vlad. "And I missed you, too," he added shyly.

"Aw, thanks," said Minxie. "But how can you ever be bored in that amazing house?"

Minxie had followed Vlad home once and she thought Misery Manor was the coolest place she'd ever seen.

Vlad pulled a face. "Mother spent all weekend making me practise my vamp— my skills," he corrected himself. He looked around anxiously but there was nobody there to hear.

Minxie didn't seem to care whether anyone was listening. "That's AWESOME!" she said. "What did you do? Did you learn how to change into a werewolf?"

Vlad looked horrified. "NO!" he cried. Then lowering his voice, he said, "No one does that these days – that's an *ancient* vampire skill. We just change into bats so we can get around quicker."

Minxie looked disappointed. "Oh," she said. Then she asked, "What about chopping off people's heads? Did you do that?"

"Minxie, shhh!" Vlad grabbed her arm. "Please don't say such horrid things."

Minxie laughed. "I was only teasing. I know you aren't like that any more – I just read about it in a book I found in the library. It's called *Fangs for the Memories*."

Vlad chuckled. "It sounds silly," he said.

Minxie shrugged. "It says it's written by a real vampire like you and it's all about his life. I thought it might help me understand you better."

Vlad felt a warm glow spread through him as he thought of the effort Minxie had gone to.

"It's so good to be here with you," he said, grinning. "It's much more fun than being with Mother and Father. Not that I will be for much longer," he added, his face falling.

"Why's that?" Minxie asked.

"They want to send me to Transylvania to learn how to be a real *you-know-what…*" Vlad tailed off.

"WHOA!" Minxie shouted, holding up her hands. "Stop right there! You're going to TRANSYLVANIA? WITHOUT ME?"

"Not if I can help it," Vlad said. "But they might make me go, whether I like it or not.

I need to figure out how to change Mother and Father's minds. And I've only got two weeks until they come back from their trip." He sighed.

"Your mum and dad have gone away? WHOOO!" Minxie punched the air with her free hand. "You know what this means?" she said. "I can come to your house whenever I want!"

Vlad's heart gave a little leap – whether from fear or excitement he wasn't quite sure. It would be fantastic to have Minxie to come and play but…

"Grandpa and Mulch are still at home," he said.

"They won't mind," said Minxie confidently, linking her arm through Vlad's.

The bell rang and they headed off to the playground to join the rest of their class who were lining up to go inside, chattering noisily.

Their teacher, Miss Lemondrop, called for the children to settle down. She seemed to be in an especially happy mood this morning.

"Go to your desks quickly and quietly when you get inside, please!" she called out above the children's chatter. "I have an exciting announcement to make."

Minxie looked at Vlad and grinned.

I'm so glad to be back at school! Vlad thought happily.

3

Vlad was completely relaxed as he followed
the others into the classroom and found his
place next to Minxie. He didn't have to think
about Transylvania or mind-control skills or
his other vampire tasks while he was in class.
He could just settle down at his desk and
enjoy the day.

He smiled to himself as he got out the
pens and pencils Minxie had lent him.
Even the stationery was better at human
school – no rough parchment or scratchy
quills and inkpots.

Miss Lemondrop came over as Vlad was neatly laying out his things. "I must have a word with your parents, Vlad," she said. "They haven't signed the letter I gave you when you first arrived.

We need your address for the school records. Will they be fetching you today?"

"No," Vlad murmured.

"They've gone to Transylvania," said Minxie.

"Thank you, Minxie," said Miss Lemondrop. "I think Vlad can tell me himself."

"Minxie's right," said Vlad. "Mother hasn't been there for centur— I mean years and years," he corrected himself. "Father has taken her as a treat. They're staying with my auntie Pavlova."

"That's lovely," said Miss Lemondrop, beaming. Then her face clouded with worry. "If your parents are away, who's looking after you?" she asked.

"Grandpa," Vlad said.

"Perfect!" Miss Lemondrop said. "I'll talk to him instead. I'd like to tell him how well you've been doing."

Vlad went cold. She couldn't meet Grandpa!

Luckily Minxie jumped in to save him by saying, "Vlad's coming to mine for tea tonight. I'll make sure he tells his grandpa that you want to see him when he comes to fetch him from my house."

Miss Lemondrop smiled. "That's very

kind, Minxie."

Vlad still felt a little bit sick. He could tell that Miss Lemondrop was not going to rest until she had met his family.

At least he was safe for now, he told himself – Miss Lemondrop seemed to believe Minxie's explanation.

The teacher bustled back to the front of the class and called for silence with her usual, "One … two … three!"

Once everyone was quiet she said, "Good morning, Badger Class!"

All together, the class replied, "Good morning, Miss Lemondrop."

"This morning I have some very special news for you." She picked up a piece of paper from her desk and peered at it through her spectacles. "Mrs Viola has asked us to put on a show in front of the whole school," she said. Then she read from the note: "'Badger Class will perform their own interpretation of the fairy tale *Hansel and Gretel* on the Friday evening before the half-term holiday. There will be a part for everyone in the class but auditions for the main roles will be held next week. Please sign up on the list in the hall tomorrow afternoon. The auditions will be next Monday, so you have a whole week to prepare your audition pieces.'"

The class erupted into excited chatter.

Minxie tapped Vlad on the arm. "I think you'll get a main part, Vlad. You're an awesome actor!"

Vlad blushed. "Thanks," he said. On his first day at school, he had impersonated his parents and Grandpa Gory and told some jokes that everyone had loved. Everyone, that is, except a boy called Boz – the naughtiest boy in the class.

"You'd be an amazing Hansel," Minxie said.

"No way!" said a voice from behind Vlad. "*I* always get the big parts."

Vlad knew without looking round that the voice belonged to Boz.

"Boswell Jones!" Miss Lemondrop called out sharply. "No one gets to choose their role. Mr Bendigo and

Mrs Viola will decide based on the auditions.
I am sure they will be very fair," she added in
a kinder tone.

The rest of the day went well for Vlad –
so well that he didn't want it to end. His
favourite bit had been when Miss Lemondrop
took the class to the school library in the
afternoon. She'd told the children to each
choose a book. Vlad had found a series of
stories called *The Secret Six*.
They were adventure books
about a group of six friends
who lived by the sea. Vlad
chose *The Secret Six Find Some
Treasure!* Miss Lemondrop said
that for homework the class
should write a report on the
book they had chosen. This was the kind of

task Vlad knew he could be good at.

Not like the things Mother makes me do, he thought as he and Minxie walked to the bike shed after school had finished.

It really had been a lovely day. Even going home would not be as bad as usual, now that his parents were away. Vlad thought of how he could curl up in his coffin with the book when he got home and then have a little snooze before Grandpa and Mulch woke up.

"What are you thinking about?" Minxie asked. "You look as if you're daydreaming."

Vlad looked at Minxie.

"I was just thinking about how happy I am. You were great, talking to Miss Lemondrop this morning," he added. "I don't know how to thank you."

Minxie twisted her face into a thoughtful expression. "We-ell," she said slowly. "Since you mention it, I've been thinking…"

She wiggled her eyebrows up and down in a mysterious manner. "I think it would be EPIC if I came to your house for a sleepover!"

Vlad's forehead crinkled. "No … that wouldn't work," he said.

"Why not?" Minxie asked, her hands on her hips.

"Because—" Vlad stopped himself and glanced round to make sure no one was listening. Then he leaned towards Minxie and said quietly, "Vampires sleep in the *day*. You wouldn't want to do that, would you?"

Minxie roared with laughter. "Of course not!" she said. "I'd come over to yours for tea and then I'd stay the night. That's how sleepovers work. It's not about *sleeping*, in any case. A sleepover is mostly midnight feasts and watching films and chatting and…"

The more Minxie said, the more horrified

Vlad became. "No! Night-time is the *worst* time for you to come to my house," he said.

Minxie pursed her lips in thought. "Even though your parents are in Transylvania?"

"So?" said Vlad.

"If your parents aren't there, how can it be dangerous for me to come over?" she asked.

"But Grandpa and Mulch are still there," Vlad said. "I still have to wait until they're asleep before I sneak out."

"So? They'll be asleep when I come after school, too, won't they?" Minxie said.

Vlad groaned. "But you said you wanted to stay for the *night*, which is when they wake up. What if they come into my room? Then what will you do?"

"Easy," said Minxie. "I'll hide! You've already told me that your grandpa falls asleep so much he doesn't know what you're doing half the time. And Mulch has his jobs to do.

It'll be fine!"

Minxie did seem to have it all worked out, Vlad thought. And it would be fun having her to stay for the night. But he was still very nervous – his parents would be furious if they ever found out he had invited a human to the house! Then again, if he was very careful they wouldn't ever find out…

Minxie could see that Vlad was wavering. "If you do invite me, I'll bring chocolate and marshmallows and all kinds of stuff," she said.

The little vampire could feel his mouth beginning to water. "That does sound good," he admitted. "I only ever get blood at home and I hate it."

They'd reached the bike shed but Minxie wasn't going to give up.

"Shall I come home with you now?" she suggested. "We could practise stuff for the

49

audition – cos I was thinking, if you are Hansel, I could be Gretel!"

"Tell you what," he said, "I'll have a think about it tonight. Then perhaps we can make a plan tomorrow, OK?"

Minxie opened her mouth to protest, but Vlad was already thinking $B - A - T$!

"No – Vlad, wait!" cried Minxie.

Too late.

POOF! Vlad was a bat again, high in the sky, and flying away from Minxie and the school.

4

Vlad turned back into his vampire form in the graveyard of Misery Manor and hurriedly changed out of his uniform, stashing it under the yew tree. Then he ran to the front door, opening and closing it as quietly as he could.

Flit was in the hall, flying around in excited circles.

"Thank goodness you're back safely! I've been waiting for you. Did you have a good day? Let's go back to your room – I want to hear all about it." Then he paused, flicking his large ears in the direction of the staircase.

"What is it, Flit?" asked Vlad. He could tell that Flit had picked up a noise with his super-sharp bat hearing.

"Someone's calling your name!" Flit's eyes grew wide in panic.

Vlad squashed himself up against the dark wallpaper and clutched his cape around him, praying the shadows would hide him.

After a few minutes, he was able to hear the voice, too. It was coming closer.

"Vlad? Vladimir?"

Grandpa!

Why was Grandpa Gory awake? The sun was still in the sky.

Maybe I should turn into a bat and fly straight past him, Vlad thought. But it was too late – Grandpa was already on the landing.

"Is that you, Vlad?" he called.

Vlad wanted to say "No!" but he knew that, although Grandpa was short-sighted, he was

not stupid.

"Yes, it's me," Vlad said wearily.

"Where've you been?" Grandpa demanded, shaking his walking stick. "I went to check on you and you weren't in your room. You mustn't go wandering off without telling me. You might get eaten by werewolves."

Vlad couldn't help grinning in spite of his grandpa's cross tone of voice. He knew there were no werewolves near Misery Manor.

"I'm responsible for you while your parents are away," Grandpa continued. He took a few shaky steps. As he moved out of the gloom he was illuminated by the light from the candles on the wall.

Vlad saw then, with a stab of guilt, that his grandfather looked more anxious than angry. His huge eyebrows were knitted together in concern.

"What in hell's bells would I do if you went missing? What would I tell them?"

"Grandpa, it's all right," Vlad said.

"Don't worry, Gory," squeaked Flit, flying into view. "I was helping him practise for his Bat Licence."

"That's right," said Vlad, glancing at Flit for encouragement. "I was learning some new moves."

Grandpa was leaning heavily against the banister. He looked very tired, Vlad realized.

"Well, you'd better save your flying for later," Grandpa said. "I'm glad to hear you've been practising, but... Wait a minute!" the old vampire exclaimed, catching a glimpse of the sunlight shining in through the keyhole in the front door. "You weren't OUTSIDE, were you?"

"Uh-oh..." said Flit.

"W-we only went out for a second," Vlad stammered.

Grandpa came down the stairs as quickly as he could, muttering and spluttering and wheezing and puffing.

Vlad shivered. He was used to his parents getting furious about the slightest little thing

55

but he'd never seen Grandpa this angry before.

Grandpa hobbled over to Vlad then stopped and waved his stick in the air, shouting, "You must NEVER, EVER go out in the light, young vampire! It's *very* dangerous. As for you, Flit," he added, "you should know better—"

"But I'm fine, Grandpa," Vlad insisted. "Look – not frazzled."

Vlad knew that the most important rules of Vampire Health and Safety were "No Sun, No Sun and No Sun" because his mother had told him many times. However, since he'd been to school in the daytime more than once now, and hadn't been hurt at all, he was beginning to question the rules.

Grandpa was still cross, though. "It's not only being frazzled you have to worry about, young devil!" he was saying. "Think what

would happen if a human saw you! You know how much humans hate us."

"Yes," said Vlad. "But why, Grandpa?" he added.

"That is a very good question," said Grandpa. "It's all to do with how our ancestors used to behave, back when I was a young vampire…" He began to relax as he always did when he started telling stories about the olden days.

Usually Vlad found these tales extremely boring but this time he listened carefully.

"Humans have always been frightened of us because of our love of blood," Grandpa Gory went on. "We used to bite humans and suck their blood right out of them, you see."

Vlad shuddered. "I know," he said. "But we don't do that any more. We have our blood delivered in a van by Red Cells Express."

Gory sighed. "True, but humans don't realize how much we've changed. Think how fascinating it'd be for us and them if we could make *friends* with human beings!" Grandpa chuckled.

If only you knew! Vlad thought.

"I'd love to study a real live human – much more interesting than a griffin or a phoenix. I could write an appendix for the *Encyclopedia of Curious Creatures*. Now, I remember when…"

"Grandpa!" Vlad interrupted. "I'm a bit tired after my flying. Can I go to my coffin?"

"Certainly not!" cried Gory, looking suddenly cross again. "You're to come and have some breakfast where I can keep an eye on you. Come with me to the kitchen and Mulch will fix you something."

Vlad looked for Flit, hoping the little bat would get him out of this, but Flit had fallen asleep, hanging upside down from the chandelier. He had no choice but to follow Grandpa out of the hallway and down the back stairs.

Vlad had only been down to the basement where Mulch lived a couple of times and that had been a long time ago. Mulch always brought meals upstairs to the dining room and Mortemia and Drax had made it clear that Mulch was not to be disturbed while he worked. Vlad had never liked the basement in any case. It was even darker and damper than the rest of Misery Manor. There were no candles to light the way down and the walls were cold and clammy to the touch.

Vlad shuddered as he clutched his cape around him. Then he slowly followed Grandpa down the stone steps and into the gloom beyond.

5

When he entered Mulch's kitchen, Vlad had a lovely surprise.

"Wow!" he said, taking in the colourful cups and plates, the checked tablecloth and the roaring fire. "It's so cosy in here – I don't remember it being like this."

Mulch beamed. "I'm glad you like it, Master Impaler," he said. "I thought the old place could do with cheering up. But where have you been?" he said, his smile giving way to a frown. "I heard from Master Gory that you weren't in your room. Not going outside

before the sun has set, I hope?" He fixed Vlad with a serious stare. "That's extremely dangerous."

"Exactly what I said." Grandpa wheezed. Then the old vampire's wrinkled face softened and broke into a cheeky grin. "Make us some hot chocolate, can you, Mulch?"

Mulch's heavy frown also cleared and he smiled, too. "Certainly, Master Gory."

"*What?*" Vlad exclaimed. He was so surprised that he forgot to be scared. "But Mother and Father don't like—"

Grandpa turned, his toothy grin flashing in the candlelight. "Ah, but they're not here, are they? I told you – I'm in charge now."

Vlad didn't know what to think as he sat down at the huge oak table. He had often wondered why Mulch had a kitchen, considering all he ever had to do was to pour blood into tall glasses. But now he knew!

Mulch went over to a large white fridge and pulled out a jug, then fetched a purple tin and three mugs from a cupboard. He took them over to the open fire and poured some liquid from the jug into a small cauldron that was hanging over the flames.

"Our little secret," said Grandpa, tapping his nose with his finger.

Mulch turned and gave a very slow wink. "Your grandfather and I like to sit in here by the fire and have a chat – when we can," he said. "Take a seat, Master Gory," he added, pulling out a rocking chair.

Grandpa sank into the chair with a contented noise. He shut his eyes and began rocking back and forth. Meanwhile Mulch removed the lid from the tin and spooned some dark powder into the saucepan, then stirred the mixture.

A delicious smell filled the room. After a few moments, the liquid began to steam and Mulch poured the drink into the mugs.

"Don't forget the marshmallows!" Gory said.

Vlad had to pinch himself. *I must be dreaming*, he thought. This was just like what

Minxie had told him about human midnight feasts!

But he wasn't dreaming – a first sip of the chocolatey drink assured him of that.

"How…? Why…?" Vlad couldn't find the words to ask the questions he wanted answers to.

Grandpa said, "We're not here to talk about hot chocolate, Vlad. We have more important things to discuss." He tried to look stern but with chocolate dripping from his top lip, he only looked funny. "Such as you promising me *never* to go out flying while there's even the *tiniest* bit of sun left in the sky."

Vlad paused. He didn't want to lie.
If I don't say the words "I promise", then maybe it's OK, he thought.

"All right," he said.

Grandpa looked doubtful for a second, then he licked his lips. "Good. Because if a human were ever to see you, I don't like to think what they'd do to you. You might end up in prison – or worse…" he tailed off.

Vlad desperately wanted to avoid having a conversation about humans. "This drink is delicious!" he said, hoping to distract his grandpa. But it didn't work.

"Do you remember my old friend Vesuvius Glare, Mulch?" Grandpa said. "*He* went out flying just as the sun was setting … and do you know what happened to *him*, Vlad?"

"He was caught by a human?" Vlad asked.

"No," said Grandpa. He leaned forward in his rocking chair and then shouted, "FRAZZLED!"

Vlad jumped.

Mulch put a large hand on Vlad's shoulder.

"Don't worry, Master Impaler," he said. "Glare was all right – just a little singed at the edges. But he never flew again," he said, his voice taking on a gloomier tone. "As long as you don't get carried away with thoughts of *storybook adventures*…" Mulch held Vlad's gaze for a little longer than was necessary.

Vlad shifted uncomfortably. He knew that Mulch was hinting at the fact that he had found Vlad's human storybook hidden in his bedroom the week before. He wasn't about to give the game away to Grandpa, was he?

Vlad needn't have worried. Mulch gave him another slow wink, then he straightened up and said to Grandpa, "Didn't you have something else to say to the young master, Sir?"

Grandpa looked blank.

"The letter?" Mulch said.

"Oh, yes. It's from your mother." Grandpa

put his hand into the top pocket of his velvet dinner jacket and pulled out a piece of parchment.

"Already?" said Vlad.

"Yes, it had just arrived by Bat Express when I found you in the hall. They've had a change of plan."

Vlad froze. "They don't want me to go to Transylvania right now after all, do they?" he asked.

"No, no," said Grandpa, fishing out a monocle from his pocket. He held the parchment at arm's length. "She's just bringing us up to date on their plans. She tells me that they're having a thoroughly evil time in Transylvania and that she has met your cousin Lupus. She says he is 'certainly a bad young vampire' and that he will 'teach you how to behave'. She hopes that you have been working hard, and says that she's persuaded Drax to come home early as she is worried about your tasks and wants to check up on you. They'll be flying back at the end of this week—"

"WHAT?" Vlad cried. "That's too early! I haven't even started the tasks yet."

"Indeed," said Gory. "Which is why there must be no more time-wasting – we need to start now." He got up from his chair. "When I was a young vampire we had no need of lessons in mind control," he began. "You simply thought of the thing you wanted to happen and it happened. But you young vampires seem to be losing your natural vampiric abilities. I don't know what the world is coming to, in my day…"

Vlad didn't know if it was the sound of Grandpa's voice…

Or the warmth of the hot chocolate filling his belly…

Or the darkness of Mulch's kitchen…

But he was finding it harder and harder to concentrate…

He felt as though the walls were closing in on him…

And the room was getting darker and darker…

Then someone was calling his name.

"Vlad? Vlad, are you listening?"

"Sorry, Miss Lemondrop!" Vlad cried.

"WHO? WHAT?"

Vlad sat up with a start. He must have fallen asleep!

"*Who* is Miss Lemondrop?" Grandpa asked suspiciously.

"I-I don't know," Vlad said, crossing his fingers inside his cape.

"And what's this?" Grandpa asked, bending over creakily.

Before Vlad could stop him, his grandfather had picked up his school library copy of *The Secret Six Find Some Treasure!* and was waving it in his face.

Vlad gasped. It must've fallen from his cape when he'd nodded off!

"I-I don't know where that came from," he squeaked.

He closed his eyes and waited for the
explosion which he was sure would follow
once Grandpa realized that his grandson
had been reading a human storybook. He
held his breath as he listened to Grandpa
Gory muttering to himself and flicking
through the pages. Then he heard Grandpa
say something very surprising indeed.

"This is rather good, Mulch," he said.

Vlad opened one eye. His grandpa was

beaming! Vlad opened his other eye and let out the breath he'd been holding.

"Yes, yes," Gory was saying, scanning the pages of the story. "Not a patch on the *Encyclopedia of Curious Creatures*, but it would be useful for research, actually."

"I think I recognize that book, Master," Mulch said slowly. "I've seen it among some of the older books in the library – when I was dusting."

Vlad couldn't believe his luck! Mulch and Grandpa were much less strict than his mother and father. Maybe Minxie was right and he *could* get away with inviting her for a sleepover after all...

Grandpa sat up suddenly and passed the book back to Vlad. "But you haven't got time for reading, have you! Oh, badness me!" He shuddered. "We must concentrate on getting your mind-control skills up to scratch,

my young devil. Fun's over," he declared, brushing his hands together. "To work!"

And with that, all the hopefulness Vlad had been feeling vanished in an instant.

Vlad spent all night practising mind control with Grandpa Gory. They started with a marshmallow.

"See if you can move that from the bowl into your mug," Grandpa said. "Should be easy – it's as light as a feather, after all."

Vlad focused on the marshmallow. Then he closed his eyes and thought about how soft and fluffy the sweet was. He tried to think of it rising in the air, floating up like a mini cloud and hovering over his mug… But then he saw his mother's face before

him, frowning. He heard her say, "You are a terrible vampire. You can't even lift something as light as this!" He thought about her coming home early and being so angry that he had to leave immediately for Transylvania...

He opened his eyes.

Mulch and Grandpa were looking awkwardly at one another.

"Did it move?" Vlad asked hopefully. "Even just a tiny bit?"

"Er, no. I'm afraid not," said Grandpa. "Why don't we try with a spider's web? That's even lighter."

"Good idea," said Mulch. "There's one over there by the cupboard. See if you can move it over to the table."

Vlad stared hard at the cobweb. Then he closed his eyes and thought about it floating across the kitchen. This should be easy – he knew that cobwebs were as light as gossamer. They were so light that when you brushed against them they tickled your skin.

"Urgh!" he shouted, his eyes snapping wide open. The very thought of touching a cobweb had convinced him that it was on his hand! He flicked at his hand where it tickled but there was nothing there.

"Oh dear," said Grandpa Gory, looking very disappointed.

"But I felt it on my skin!" Vlad protested.

Mulch looked embarrassed. "I think that's what you call having an overactive imagination, Master Impaler," he said. "Why don't you try persuading Flit to fly down here with the power of your mind?" he suggested. "As you and he get on so well, there might be a stronger link between you. It might be easier than starting with an object."

Grandpa agreed.

And so Vlad tried and tried to summon Flit. He closed his eyes and imagined calling Flit by name; he pictured the bat waking up and picking up the signal. He even visualized Flit doing loop-the-loops with excitement as he entered the kitchen and saw how cosy it was.

Again – nothing happened.

Eventually dawn broke and Grandpa went to his coffin in a huff, muttering that Vlad might as well start packing for Transylvania right away.

Vlad ran up to his room and collapsed into his coffin, desperate to forget about his failings as a vampire. He just wanted to fall asleep and then go to human school again where he was actually good at things and had a friend his own age.

Instead he tossed and turned, his mind full of anxiety. He couldn't get to sleep for ages.

When he woke, he checked the pocket watch.

He had overslept!

"It's a quarter to nine!" he gasped in horror. "Flit! I'm going to be late," he called to his pet bat as he scrambled out of his

coffin and hurried to put on his cape. "Why didn't you wake me? Flit?"

The little bat hovered around Vlad nervously. "I'm sorry!" he squeaked. "I overslept, too! I was so worried about you yesterday that I didn't sleep properly in the daytime. I was exhausted when I finally nodded off."

"I hope I won't get into trouble at school for being late," Vlad said, his voice panicky. "It's bad enough getting into trouble at home!"

"Fly safely!" Flit squeaked, as Vlad hurtled out of the door.

Vlad crept through the manor as quickly
and quietly as he could. As soon as he was
outside, he sprinted through the graveyard to
the yew tree. He changed into his uniform,
then he morphed into bat form and whizzed
to school.

He rushed through the empty playground
to the bike shed and transformed back into
his vampire self. Then he dashed to hang up
his cape and get to the classroom.

When he got there, everyone was already
sitting at their desks.

"Ah, there you are, Vlad. Minxie was
telling me that she thought you were sick
this morning. Are you sure you're all right?"
the teacher asked.

"Y-yes, I'm sorry. I thought I was poorly
but I'm OK now," Vlad said. He shot a glance

at Minxie who mouthed, "Don't worry!"

"Good. Have you got a note from your grandpa for being late?" Miss Lemondrop asked.

"Ah – I…" Vlad felt something prodding at his hands in his lap. He looked down and saw a piece of paper with writing in shaky letters:

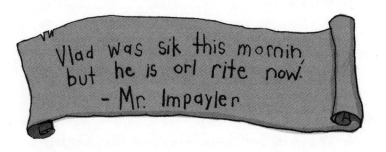

Vlad was sik this mornin, but he is orl rite now.
- Mr. Impayler

Vlad glanced at Minxie again but she was staring straight ahead.

"Ah, yes – here's a note," said Vlad, handing it to the teacher.

"Your grandfather has very, um, unusual spelling, doesn't he?" Miss Lemondrop said, once she had read it.

Vlad nodded. "He still finds writing in English quite tricky."

"Of course," said Miss Lemondrop kindly. "I wouldn't have a clue how to write a note in Transylvanian." She laughed. "Now, as I was saying, today we are learning about the life cycle of a frog. Who knows what a baby frog looks like?"

Boz shouted out, "Small and green and slimy. Like snot!"

The class giggled.

Miss Lemondrop's expression darkened but her voice remained calm. "No calling out, please, Boswell."

"Don't be silly, Boz," said Minxie. "Everyone knows a baby frog is a tadpole. And they're not green and slimy," she added. "They're black and wriggly."

"Like your boyfriend in his stupid cape," said Boz, under his breath.

Miss Lemondrop didn't hear what Boz said but Vlad did. He wished he knew how to stop Boz from being so mean.

"Well done, Minxie," the teacher said. "I've brought some real tadpoles to show you. Look." She reached down behind her and lifted a small fish tank on to her desk. It was full of water and green pondweed.

"Line up at the front," said the teacher. "Quietly and sensibly!" she added, as everyone rushed to be first.

"Cool!" said Ravi. "They really ARE black and wriggly."

"They look like commas," said Leisha.

Miss Lemondrop laughed. "Very good," she said. They'd been learning about commas in their story-writing classes.

Vlad was wary of the tadpoles. "Can they jump?" he asked.

Boz snorted. "Of course not. They haven't got any legs, dummy!" He pushed his way to the front and leaned over the top of the tank. Before the teacher could stop him, Boz had dipped his fingers into the water and scooped up a tadpole. Then he threw it at Vlad. "They can fly, though!" he shouted, bursting into laughter as the tadpole hit Vlad smack on the nose.

Some of the class screamed as Vlad swatted frantically at his face. "Get it off me!" he cried.

Miss Lemondrop was horrified. "Go and sit down at once, Boswell!" she commanded, reaching to pick the little tadpole off her desk,

where it had landed.

He's such a bully, Vlad thought. He had never felt so cross with someone before. All at once he wished that the tadpoles would ALL leap out of the tank and land right on Boz's head. That'd stop him from pushing people and being rude.

Vlad stared hard at the tadpoles. Then he closed his eyes and pictured them gathering together into a black wriggly mass…

He imagined them whispering to each other…

Then he thought about them LEAPING out of the water…

Through the air…

And landing right on top of Boz's head!

Suddenly there was a huge commotion.

Vlad opened his eyes to see Boz shouting and swiping at his head. "URGH! They're slimy!" he yelled.

Children were screaming and running back to their seats. Only Minxie stayed by Vlad's side.

"HELP!" shrieked Boz.

Vlad stood stock-still, staring at Boz – whose head was covered in tiny, wriggling tadpoles!

"Did you do that?" Minxie whispered to Vlad, her eyes wide.

Vlad's throat was dry. *Had* he done it? Maybe all that mind-control practice with Grandpa had paid off… But what if he was found out?

Vlad needn't have worried. Miss Lemondrop was far too busy telling Boz off to suspect a thing.

"What a cruel thing to do, Boswell!" Miss Lemondrop cried. She was picking the tadpoles out of Boz's hair and putting them back in the tank. "Those poor creatures will be very upset. It's bad enough that you threw one at Vlad. Why do you always have to be the centre of attention?"

"But it wasn't me!" Boz shouted. He whirled round to point at Vlad. "It was HIM! The freaky Transylvanian boy did it."

"Don't be rude!" Minxie said.

"Minxie is absolutely right," said Miss Lemondrop. "We're not unkind about different cultures in this school, are we? In any case, we saw you flick one at Vlad. You'd better go and see Mrs Viola at break and explain yourself, Boswell."

When the bell for break time rang, everyone got out of their seats and ran to the playground. Boz pushed past Vlad on his way to see the Head Teacher, Mrs Viola.

"You'd better watch out, freak," he whispered. "I *know* you did that. I'll get my own back – just you wait."

Vlad's heart was pumping hard. His head felt so full of worries, he thought it might burst.

He was such a ball of nerves that he had to go and find a shady spot under a tree where he could sit down on his own for a while. Minxie didn't leave him alone for long though.

"Boz really upset you, didn't he?" she said, sitting down with him. "Look, don't worry. Mrs Viola will give him a rocket!"

"That will make him even noisier and more dangerous than ever," said Vlad.

Minxie giggled. "You are funny!" she said. "It means that she'll tell him off so much that he'll feel as though she has shot him into outer space in a rocket."

"Oh," said Vlad. "I wish she really *could* do that. It's bad enough that my parents are going to send me to Transylvania without having Boz hate me as well."

"Cheer up," said Minxie. "We've got the auditions to look forward to."

Vlad looked glummer than ever. "I don't think I'll be any good," he said. "I don't even know what *Hansel and Gretel* is about."

Minxie put an arm round him. "I'll tell you!" she said. "It's about a boy called Hansel

and a girl called Gretel. They are brother and sister and their wicked stepmother sends them into the forest because she doesn't want them to live with her. They meet a witch who has a gingerbread house covered in sweets and they are so hungry they start to eat the sweets – and then the witch tries to eat them."

Vlad looked horrified. "It sounds awful!" he said.

Minxie grinned. "It's not, though – Hansel and Gretel defeat the witch by being clever and brave. Just like you defeated Boz with the tadpoles," she added, with a knowing look.

Vlad blushed but he didn't say anything. He wasn't sure that he really *had* made the tadpoles jump and he didn't want Minxie to start getting crazy ideas about how he could use mind control at school.

"OK," he said. "It sounds like a great story. I'll sign up for the auditions with you."

The day ended on a much happier note.

The pupils left the classroom chattering excitedly as they ran to sign up for the auditions.

"Come on, Vlad," Minxie said, grabbing his hand and pulling him out of the classroom.

"B-but I don't know if I'll be good enough," Vlad said.

"Of course you will!" Minxie replied. "You'll be better than good – you'll be brilliant. And you'll love it!"

"What if I can't get to all the rehearsals? If they're after school I might not be able to come. I have to get home early so that I can sleep before Grandpa wakes me up for my vampire lessons."

"There's no point in worrying about that

yet," Minxie said, looking almost as stern as Mortemia. "First of all we have to get a part! Come on, let's go."

"OK," said Vlad, and off they ran. He *was* excited about the show. Minxie was right – he had never felt so happy as when he was up in front of the class, making people laugh with his jokes. He decided to stop worrying and enjoy himself.

When they reached the hall Mr Bendigo was there and a small group of children were crowded around the sheets that were pinned up on one of the boards. Ravi and Leisha were looking at the different roles in the play.

"I'd like to be the father," said Ravi. "He's a woodcutter." He began miming chopping down trees.

"Very good," said Mr Bendigo, smiling.

"What role are you going to audition for, Minxie?" asked Ravi.

"I'm going to go for Gretel," said Minxie. "What about you, Leesh?"

"I want to be the evil stepmother," said Leisha, "cos I'm awesome at doing a cackling laugh!" She gave a loud and screechy demonstration.

"Ow! Save that for the audition, Leisha," said Mr Bendigo, making a show of covering his ears. "I'd like to keep my eardrums in good working order tonight!"

Everyone laughed and began chatting noisily about the other parts in the play while Minxie pulled Vlad with her to the front of the group.

Her face fell as she saw the names. "Oh no!" she said. "Boz has already signed up to play Hansel!"

"Don't worry, you can audition for Hansel, too, Malika," said Mr Bendigo, handing her a pen. "That's the whole point of an audition – we have to choose the best person for the part. We might have ten people trying out for Hansel – who knows? We'll see you all perform on Monday next week at the auditions, and then I'll discuss with Mrs Viola who we think is right."

"It's not *me* that wants to be Hansel," said Minxie. "I want to be Gretel. It's VLAD that's going to be Hansel." She took the pen from the teacher and wrote her name under

the role of Gretel and in the column for Hansel she wrote Vlad's name under Boz's.

"There," she said. "We'll show them who are the best people to be Hansel and Gretel, won't we, Vlad?"

"We will?" Vlad asked, uncertainly.

"Course!" Minxie said. "We can do our famous joke routine, can't we?" She nudged him.

Vlad hesitated. "Er, can we?" he mumbled.

"Go on," said Ravi. "Let's hear some of your jokes."

Minxie cleared her throat and said in a loud voice, "Hey, Vlad? What's a vampire's favourite dessert?"

Vlad looked horrified. Minxie was going to give him away! But he caught sight of Mr Bendigo, who was smiling encouragingly.

"We don't know," said Mr Bendigo. "What IS a vampire's favourite dessert, Vlad?"

There was no way out – Vlad was going to have to tell the truth.

"Blood," Vlad said, looking miserable.

Minxie squealed in delight. "No! The answer is 'I scream' – get it?" She giggled. "Ice cream … *I scream?*"

Vlad looked around with a puzzled expression. Everyone was smiling and laughing – no one seemed suspicious at all!

"That's a good one," Mr Bendigo said.

"I love the way you said 'blood' and then pulled that face, Vlad!" Leisha said.

"What about this one?" said Minxie. "How does Dracula like his food served?"

Vlad saw her wink at him and suddenly realized what she wanted him to do. He bent over as though he was leaning on a walking stick, and put on his Grandpa Gory voice.

"Badness me, I don't know. I've never met him," he wheezed.

"I'll tell you," said Minxie. "He likes it in BITE-sized pieces!"

Everyone laughed and Vlad was so relieved that he laughed, too. "Mwhahaha!"

"Wow. That's awesome – your laugh's as good as Leisha's cackle!" said Ravi. "You sound like a real vampire when you laugh like that."

Vlad grinned. *If only his mother had been there*

to hear that, he thought to himself.

Minxie caught his eye and said, "Do it again, Vlad! You're such a good actor. You should definitely be Hansel in the play."

Vlad hesitated, but then he threw back his head and out came the most evil laugh he had ever managed. "MWHAHAHAHAAAA!"

"That's *so* cool," said Leisha.

The other children clapped and cheered.

Vlad beamed. Maybe everything was going to be all right after all.

Vlad and Minxie left the hall and went back out into the playground. There was a breeze ruffling the leaves on the trees. Vlad loved the feel of it on his skin.

"I was worried in there," Vlad said, as he made his way across to the bike shed. "I thought for a moment that you were about to tell everyone that I'm a you-know-what."

"As *if*!" said Minxie. "I don't want anyone knowing my friend's a vampire – it's the best secret in the world. Which reminds me," she said, her eyes glinting. "Have you had a

chance to think about inviting me over for a sleepover? Pleeeeeese?" She looked at him, pleadingly.

Vlad sighed. "I really don't think I can."

Minxie pouted. "Oh," she said.

"Anyway, last night Grandpa found out that Mother and Father are coming home this Friday, which is much sooner than we thought," said Vlad. "I have so many tasks to finish before then. If I don't figure out how to do them, Mother and Father will be sure to pack me off to Transylvania right away!"

Minxie put her head on one side. "I could help you," she said. "You've already told me that your grandpa falls asleep all the time, so he'll never notice I'm there. It's perfect!"

"I don't think you can help with the kind of stuff I have to do," Vlad said.

"Try me," Minxie said.

Vlad looked around. The playground was

buzzing with noise as children played and their parents stood chatting. "Don't you have to go and get your bus?" he asked.

"Don't change the subject," said Minxie. "Tell me what you have to do."

"OK." Vlad moved closer. "I have to collect one hundred different types of spider and label them all."

Minxie clapped her hands together in delight. "Easy!" she cried. "What else?"

Vlad hesitated. "Well, you know what happened with the tadpoles?"

Minxie's hand flew to her mouth. "It *was* you!" she gasped. "I knew it was! I read in *Fangs for the Memories* that vampires can use their minds to move things and control other people – is that what you did?"

"Shh!" Vlad looked around again to check no one had heard. "I *think* I did," he admitted. "But the weird thing is, I was

practising all night with Grandpa and I couldn't do it."

"Well, you can now! So that's one thing you can cross off the list already – which means I *can* come to your house."

"Oooooh! Minxie's going to Vlad's house," said a sneering voice.

"Boz!" Minxie whipped round. The wind caught her hair and blew it into her face.

Boz sniggered.

"Are you spying on us?" Minxie demanded, pushing her hair away.

"What if I am?" said Boz, pulling a face. "It's all HIS fault that I have to stay behind after school." He glared at Vlad and took a step towards him. "Mrs Viola says I have to be on Tidy-Up Duty because of what happened with the tadpoles, which is NOT FAIR." He prodded Vlad sharply in the chest.

Vlad staggered and fell back. He bashed

himself against a rubbish bin that was stuffed
with empty drink cartons and banana skins
from break time.

"Ow!" he said, rubbing his back. "That was
mean."

"So are you," said Boz, sticking out his
tongue.

Minxie drew herself up tall and took a
step towards Boz.

He tried to back away but Minxie circled
him, forcing him to walk backwards as she
approached him menacingly.

"Listen," Minxie said. "Vlad never threw
those tadpoles. You were the one with your
fingers in the water."

"I didn't even touch them!"
Boz protested. He was walking
away from Minxie, towards
Vlad. "One minute they were
in the water, the next they were

in my hair. And HE was right behind me." Boz jabbed his thumb in Vlad's direction.

Vlad could feel anger rising up in him again. He knew that Boz was right about the tadpoles on his head but *he* had started it by flicking one at Vlad. In any case, Boz was always so horrible to him. He'd picked on Vlad from the first moment he had arrived at the school.

Vlad frowned and wished Boz would stop picking on him and go away. He stepped to one side, closing his eyes as the breeze blew hair into his face. He found himself wishing so hard that Boz would go away that suddenly an image of Boz being swept up by a big gust of wind appeared in his mind.

The next thing Vlad knew, there was a yell from Boz. "What's happening?" he cried.

Vlad opened his eyes to see that Boz had been picked up by the wind and was being hurled backwards...

…right into the rubbish bin!

"Urgh!" Boz shouted, picking a banana skin off his arm.

Mr Bendigo came running over. "Boswell Jones – up to your silly tricks again," he said, reaching over to pull the boy out. "If you think this is funny, you've got another think coming. You'll be on Tidy-Up Duty for the rest of the term at this rate."

"No!" cried Boz. "That way I'd miss auditions AND rehearsals."

"You should've thought of that before you made such a spectacle of yourself," said the teacher. "That is not the way to get people's attention – you should know that by now."

"I need to go home," Vlad said to Minxie in a low voice. "Boz is going to hate me more than ever now."

Minxie was staring at him, wide-eyed. "You did it again!" she said quietly. "You controlled Boz with your mind! Oh, please let me come home with you. You could practise on me."

Vlad grabbed Minxie's arm and pulled her away from Mr Bendigo, who was now giving Boz a long and involved telling-off.

"Let me think about it some more," he said, as they walked towards the bike shed. "Maybe I could persuade Flit to distract Grandpa and Mulch."

"All right," said Minxie. "But make sure
you come up with a plan soon – we need
to practise an audition piece in time for
Monday." She waved goodbye and ran to
catch her bus.

That night, Vlad didn't have a chance to talk
to Flit before Grandpa came to get him for his
spider cataloguing. He would've preferred to
practise mind control – he was worried that he
only seemed to be able to do it when he was
feeling angry. He needed to know if he could
do it when he was in control of his feelings.
But Grandpa insisted on catching the spiders
instead.

Vlad only succeeded in catching one creepy
creature and he didn't even manage to keep it.
Its black eyes looked so scary that he dropped
it and it scurried away.

"Vladimir!" Grandpa shouted. "We are *never* going to catch one hundred spiders if you keep doing that."

"I know," Vlad said, exasperated. "But they scare me. I can't help it!"

"Well, you're going to have to learn – and fast," said Grandpa.

Vlad sighed heavily. *I won't have time to talk to Flit* or *read* The Secret Six Find Some Treasure! *now*, he thought glumly.

There was no hot chocolate with
marshmallows that night. The only good
thing that happened was that Vlad was sent
to his coffin early. This was supposed to be a
punishment but Vlad was so exhausted that
he fell asleep at once.

When morning came, he was still tired but
there was no way he was missing
school.

"I need to practise with Minxie
for the auditions," he told Flit.
"Also, I've decided to invite
her over tonight for a sleepover," he added
quickly. He knew Flit wouldn't like this idea.
He was right.

"What! Are you sure?" The bat fluttered in
front of Vlad's face but he could see that the
little vampire's mind was made up. "Well, in

that case, I'll help you to try and make
sure you don't get caught," he squeaked.

"Thanks," said Vlad. "Minxie will be
careful. We got away with it last time she
was here, remember? And as Mother and
Father aren't here, it'll be easier!"

"It would be fun to have Minxie here," Flit
admitted. "It's been very quiet with you out
at school all the time."

"You're the best, Flit!" Vlad said. He
reached up and stroked the little bat's head.
He was excited at the idea of the sleepover
but he was also very nervous. His insides
were churning worse than the first time he
tried to fly a loop-the-loop!

8

The next morning Vlad found Minxie straight away and he told her about Flit's promise to help him with the sleepover.

"This is even more exciting than the school show!" Minxie cried. "I can't WAIT! My house is so totally boring and normal. Not an amazing spooky one like yours."

"What will you tell your parents?" Vlad said.

"It's fine," Minxie replied carelessly. "I already left a note this morning to say I'd be at a sleepover. She won't check."

"But … how did you know I'd say you could come?" Vlad asked.

Minxie shrugged. "I just knew," she said, with a smile. "I can't WAIT for school to end!"

It did seem to be the longest school day ever – even for Vlad. Miss Lemondrop had set them lots of tests, which made the time pass much more slowly than usual.

At last the bell rang for the end of lessons and the children ran outside. Vlad and Minxie went to the bike shed as usual so that Vlad could change into a bat. Then something occurred to Vlad.

"I'm not going to fly today," he said. "It's not fair on you, Minxie. I'll walk with you instead."

"That's kind," said Minxie.

Then Vlad sighed. "I wish Mother and Father had a bus. Then I could drive us both home."

Minxie giggled. "You are funny, Vlad. Most humans would LOVE to be able to fly like you. And in any case, you have to have a special licence to drive a bus."

"Really?" Vlad asked. It amazed him how much Minxie seemed to know about the world.

"Of course," Minxie said. "Would YOU know how to drive one?"

"No, but I don't know anything about human life – unless I've read it in a book," Vlad added.

"Yeah, that's like me and my vampire knowledge," said Minxie. "Like, I know that if you ever eat steak, you die. I read that in *Fangs for the Memories*."

Vlad laughed. "It's not 'eat steak'," he

said. "It's if we ever get a *stake through the heart*." Then he acted as though someone had stabbed him and pretended to die a slow and agonizing death.

Minxie joined in with Vlad's laughter. "Excellent acting again!"

"Yeah, totally excellent," said a jeering voice.

Vlad turned and saw that Boz had appeared again and was walking towards them.

"When are you going to stop sneaking up on us?" Minxie demanded.

"Listen, Vlad," Boz said, ignoring Minxie, "I'm going to be Hansel – not you. All right? I always get the main part," he said. "I'm sick of you ruining everything. You should be the *witch* in the play – you've got the teeth for it!" he added, grinning nastily.

"You're not exactly a handsome prince

yourself," Minxie pointed out.

"And you should be the evil stepmother, Minxie, not Leisha," he added. "You've got weird hair – just right for the part."

Vlad was horrified as he saw Minxie's shoulders fall. She let her head drop, too. Vlad felt himself start to simmer with rage. How dare Boz be so nasty to his best friend? Minxie had never done anything to hurt Boz. He really was a horrible bully.

In that moment, Vlad found himself thinking about Boz tripping…

…and flying into the bike shed…

…and hundreds of spiders scurrying out of their webs…

…and jumping on top of Boz!

"WAAAH!" Boz shouted.

Vlad opened his eyes to see that Boz had landed in the bike shed and a whole load of spiders had fallen on to his face and into his hair.

116

"Get them off me! I HATE SPIDERS!"
Boz brushed furiously at his face, then picked
himself up and ran away, shouting and
screaming.

"Huh. What a scaredy-cat," said Minxie,
with satisfaction. "That was awesome,
though," she said, grinning. "I reckon if you
can do that, you can do anything!"

"Quick," Vlad said, picking his skateboard
out of the tangle of bikes. "Let's go while
we've got a chance."

"Yes, let's go!" cried Minxie.

When they reached the graveyard surrounding Misery Manor, Minxie and Vlad were puffing and panting from the effort of running so far.

They stopped and held on to a tombstone while they caught their breath.

"I just have to change out of my school uniform," said Vlad, making for the yew tree. Then he jumped. "What was that?" he whispered.

Something was rustling in the bushes.

"Maybe it's a ghost!" Minxie said with glee. "This is PROPERLY spooky. Are there zombies and mummies around here?"

"There's no such thing," said Vlad, brushing moss off his cape. "Thankfully," he added quietly, shuddering at the thought.

"So are we going to have a midnight feast?" Minxie said. "Does your grandpa have any *ice cream*? Hahaha!"

"No, of course not!" said Vlad impatiently. "Now we must be quiet," he added, lowering his voice as they approached the door to Misery Manor. "Grandpa might be awake. He doesn't sleep very well these days. If he appears, I'll say I was doing more flying practice and you'll have to hide. Close the door behind you, please," he added, as she slipped in.

All was deathly quiet inside. Vlad let out his breath but then suddenly there was a loud "SNOOORRRRRAAARGH!"

Minxie giggled. "Was that one of your grandpa's famous snores?" she whispered.

119

"Yes," Vlad whispered back. "Thank badness he's still asleep."

As Vlad tiptoed across the hall with Minxie close behind him, a breeze swept through, and blew out some of the candles in the chandelier.

"Where did that come from?" Vlad said. He whirled round and saw that the door was open a crack. "I thought I asked you to close the door!" he whispered, frowning at Minxie.

"I did," said Minxie, frowning back.

Vlad went to push the door shut. As he did so, he caught sight of a movement from the corner of his eye. He let out a small squeal of fright.

"What's the matter?" Minxie asked. "You've been very jumpy ever since we got here."

"S-something moved," Vlad hissed. "Over there." He pointed to a floor-length velvet curtain.

"See, I told you there's a ghooooost!" said Minxie, holding her hands up and putting on a spooky voice.

A small shape scuttled out from under the curtain and ran over Vlad's feet.

"Eeek!" he squealed again.

Minxie bent down. "It's only a spider," she said, picking up the little creature. "We could keep him for your collection."

Vlad shrank back. "Only if you hold it," he said.

Minxie dropped the spider into her pocket. "OK," she said. "But before we do anything else, I want a tour. And then we can play hide-and-seek in the graveyard," she said, counting things off on her fingers. "And then I want to spend ALL NIGHT telling spooky stories, and then—"

She was interrupted by a loud creaking noise.

"Shh!" Vlad hissed. "Someone must've woken up!"

Minxie listened. "I think you're imagining things," she said.

Sure enough, the creaking seemed to have stopped. Vlad beckoned to Minxie to follow him and they hurried along the corridor to Vlad's room in the East Wing.

"This is SO COOL," Minxie breathed.

122

"A real coffin! And LOOK at all those spiders."

Vlad shuddered. He didn't like to think how many spiders were lurking in the shadows.

"And there's Flit!" cried Minxie, pointing up to the rafters.

Flit flew down. "Hello," he said. "What are you two up to?"

"We haven't decided," said Vlad. "Flit wants to know what we're going to do," Vlad translated for Minxie.

"I know!" said Minxie. "We can practise for the auditions. I know LOADS of vampire jokes."

"Why do they all have to be vampire jokes?" Vlad asked.

"Because you're so good at pretending to be your grandpa and your dad and stuff," said Minxie. "And it's good acting that the

teachers want to see. Right." She stood up on the coffin as if it was a stage and said in a spooky voice, "What do vampires have at eleven o'clock in the morning?"

Vlad drew himself up tall and pretended to be his dad. "I like a fresh pint of blood. But what about you?"

Minxie laughed. "I prefer to have a *coffin* break!"

"Are all the jokes this bad?" Flit squeaked in bat language.

"What did he say?" Minxie asked.

"He laughed," Vlad fibbed.

"Great!" said Minxie. "Let's see if he likes this one. Why did the vampire take up acting?"

Vlad put on his best Mulch voice and said gloomily, "Because it was more fun than lying around in his coffin all the time?"

"Wrong answer!" said Minxie. "Because it was *in his blood*!"

Vlad opened his mouth to laugh but then he heard another loud CREAK from right outside the door.

"Shh!" he said.

Minxie scooted behind the coffin so that she was out of sight. She crouched low and stayed as quiet as a spider.

The creaking stopped. Vlad let out his breath and Minxie sighed.

"Isn't your house always creaky?" she asked. "I mean, it *is* very old."

"I s'pose," said Vlad. "But it's not normally *this* creaky. What if someone's followed us?"

"We would've seen them," said Minxie firmly. "Come on, I'm hungry!"

"Will you help us, Flit?" Vlad squeaked in bat language. "Could you fly ahead and warn us if Grandpa or Mulch are coming?"

"Yes! Are we going to the kitchen? I'll get some juicy grapes for me, too – I'm only

allowed them as a special treat," Flit said.

"OK," said Vlad. "But we should go quickly, the sun will be going down soon."

Vlad explained his plan to Minxie.

"Cool!" said Minxie. "It's like we're on a secret mission."

Flit flew towards the door but then immediately looped back, squeaking, "Quiet!"

Vlad and Minxie stopped in their tracks.

"There's someone out in the corridor," Flit whispered.

"Oh no!" Vlad turned to Minxie. "You're going to have to—"

"HIDE!" Flit squeaked. He flew round and round in panicky circles.

"What—?" Minxie began, but Vlad was already bundling her back in the direction of the coffin. She scrambled inside and he threw his velvet bedspread over her.

The door handle turned and the door creaked open v e r y, v e r y s l o w l y.

Vlad froze. What if it was Mulch? He said he could "smell humans" last time Minxie was at Misery Manor. And what about Grandpa? Or even worse, what if it was Mortemia or Drax, back early to surprise him?

"W-wait a minute!" Vlad cried out. "I'm … I'm just getting dressed."

"No, you're not!" said a voice. "I can see you through the keyhole." But the voice that spoke wasn't Mulch or Grandpa Gory.

The door swung open and standing there in the doorway was Boz!

9

"I *knew* there was something weird about you," Boz said. "You've been lying to us all, haven't you?"

Vlad couldn't speak. He looked around for Flit to help him, but the little bat had disappeared. Vlad swallowed hard. What was he going to do now? Boz had discovered his secret and he'd go back to school and tell everyone that Vlad was a vampire! If the teachers found out, the whole Impaler family would be sent back to Transylvania. It would be all his fault…

"You *aren't* from Transylvania," Boz said, cutting into Vlad's panicky thoughts. "You're just hiding in this battered old house. That's why Miss Lemondrop has never met your parents – because you haven't got any! You're just a poor little orphan boy with no mummy and daddy," he added in a babyish voice.

Minxie gave a strangled titter.

Boz frowned. "What was that?"

"Oh, nothing," Vlad said. "Probably just a bat – there are loads here," he said, scanning

the room again for Flit. "And spiders."

Boz shuddered.

Vlad's mind was racing. Boz hadn't guessed he was a vampire after all!

"I know I'm right," Boz said, "because you haven't got an answer, have you? You're an orphan and you should be in a special home for children with no parents. It's the law," he said importantly.

Vlad's mouth went completely dry. Boz still wanted to get his own back on him. He was going to get Vlad into trouble one way or another, unless Vlad could think of a way out of this – and fast!

"Minxie's known all about this for ages, hasn't she?" Boz went on, when Vlad didn't reply. "That's why she's been faking notes for you. Oh, I know all about that," he said, as Vlad opened his mouth to protest. "I've been on Tidy-Up Duty, remember? I found these in the library." He reached into his pocket, pulled out two crumpled pieces of paper and threw them at Vlad.

Vlad bent down and picked up the pieces of paper, then smoothed them out. They were covered in loopy handwriting – Minxie had been practising how to fake Grandpa's signature!

"It's all over for you, Mr Freaky-Teeth," said Boz. "I'm going to tell the school exactly what's going on and you'll have to leave, and I'll get to be Hansel in the show and everything'll go back to how it was before you ever arrived." He stopped to catch his breath.

Vlad tried to stay calm. He didn't know what to be more scared of – the fact that Boz had found out where he lived or the fact that he had to get Boz out of Misery Manor before Mulch and Grandpa woke up.

Even though he didn't like Boz at all, he was terrified about what would happen to him if Mulch or Grandpa found out he had got into the manor.

"You need to be quiet," Vlad said in a whisper. "Someone might hear—"

"*Who* exactly?" Boz said, sneering. "The spiders?" He raised his voice to make a point. "There's no one else in this dump!"

"Shhh!" said Vlad. But it was too late.

"Oh yes, there is," came a deep, booming voice. It echoed along the corridor of the East Wing, accompanied by a heavy STOMP-STOMP-STOMP.

Boz's expression changed from triumphant to terrified in an instant. "Wh-wh-what was that?" he gibbered.

"Now you've done it!" Vlad said. He looked around wildly for somewhere to hide Boz.

All of a sudden Minxie threw back the

bedspread. "I think you'll find that it's someone from Vlad's family. And as you weren't invited, Boz, you're going to get into trouble for being here."

STOMP-STOMP-STOMP.

Mulch was getting closer and closer!

"Minxie – what're you doing?" Vlad said through gritted fangs. "Boz won't be the only one in trouble now!"

"Eek!" cried Minxie, her face shining with excitement. "This is epic!" She dived back under the covers but made sure she could peep out of a tiny gap to see what was going on.

Boz was about to speak when Mulch appeared in the doorway, looking very stern indeed. He stepped into the room and loomed over Boz, fixing him with a terrible stare.

"What's going on?" he roared.

Boz was frozen to the spot.

"Wh-wh-what are you?" he asked.

Vlad had never seen Mulch look so
terrifying. He wanted to disappear, but instead
he told himself to use his best acting skills.

"Good evening, Mulch," he said politely.
"How are you?"

Mulch bowed. "Good evening, Master,"
he said in his normal voice. "You seem to be
having some trouble?" He took a step towards

Boz. "I don't remember the master inviting any guests."

"He's not my guest. I don't know who he is," Vlad said, trying to look brave.

"Fibber!" Boz shouted. "I go to school with—"

Vlad gasped and cried, "No!"

"It's all right, Master," Mulch said. "I'll get rid of the intruder. It's part of my job to protect you."

As he did so, Flit whizzed in through the door spluttering, "I'm sorry, Vlad! I tried to distract him!"

"AARGH! A bat!" Boz screamed, flailing out at Flit.

"Don't worry, it won't hurt you," said Mulch. "In fact," he added, with a smirk, "let me show you the way out."

Mulch began walking out of the room, with Boz kicking and squealing. As he got to

the doorway, he turned and said, "I think you should go to the dining room, Master Vlad. Unless you're not feeling particularly hungry this evening?" He looked at the lumpy shape in the coffin as he said this and winked, then turned and walked off, with Boz swinging from his fingers.

When Vlad was finally sure it was safe, he called for Minxie to come out.

She threw off the bedspread. "WOW! Mulch is COOL!" she gushed.

Flit landed on the coffin. "I agree. Mulch has certainly taught that boy a lesson. I did try to stop him coming in, but I'm glad he did now. He didn't see Minxie and he got rid of that horrible child."

"But what if Boz tells everyone at school about Mulch?" Vlad asked anxiously.

"He won't do that," said Minxie. "Didn't you see? He was TERRIFIED!"

"I hope you're right," said Vlad. "It doesn't solve my other problem though," he added. "I think Mulch *did* see you. Minxie—"

"Master?" came Mulch's voice, from the corridor.

"Mulch!" Vlad threw the bedspread over Minxie's head again. "I-I was just coming to breakfast."

"No need, Master," said Mulch, appearing in the doorway. He was carrying a tray with a large silver dome on it. He removed the dome with a flourish and said, "I thought you might like breakfast in your room after all the excitement."

"WOW!" said Vlad. "Pancakes? Hot chocolate?"

"And bacon and eggs," Mulch added, with a bow. "I thought Master could do

137

with a treat after the fright he's had. And," he added, nodding at the lump under the bedspread, "I don't think humans drink blood."

"Hmmm!" Minxie said, throwing back the covers and breathing in the delicious aromas. "Thank you, Mulch. What a perfect midnight feast!"

"My pleasure," said Mulch. "Although it's only four o'clock, actually."

Vlad was staring at the butler, his mouth wide open. "I-I don't understand," he said. "Aren't I in trouble for bringing a human home?"

"You remind me of your grandfather when he was young," Mulch said. "He has always been interested in curious creatures, too. Don't worry, I shan't tell anyone, Master Vlad." He paused. "But you'll have to promise me something."

"Anything!" said Vlad.

"You and your friend must finish all your tasks – tonight!" Mulch said. "Master Gory is getting very anxious. I'll tell him you're working hard and that you're not to be disturbed. That way, none of us will get into trouble. Deal?" he boomed.

"Deal!" said Vlad and Minxie, through mouthfuls of pancake.

10

When Friday night arrived, Vlad and Flit were in the sitting room with Grandpa after a yummy breakfast of eggs and toast. Ever since Minxie had stayed, Mulch had been giving him all sorts of delicious meals. And it wasn't just the food – he had even given Vlad time to read all of *The Secret Six Find Some Treasure!* without being disturbed. Vlad had never been happier.

That feeling was beginning to wear off now though, as he knew that all the treats and fun would have to stop the moment

his parents came home. Vlad sighed as he watched Grandpa snoozing contentedly in his armchair.

At least I have a few more minutes of freedom to finish my book report for Miss Lemondrop, he thought.

All too soon, Vlad heard voices in the hall.

"Quick!" Flit squeaked from Vlad's shoulder. "The report!"

Vlad nodded and hastily stuffed it in the inside pocket of his cape, just as his mother and father swept into the room.

"Good evening, Vladimir," said Drax, bowing formally to his son.

"Hello, Father. Hello, Mother," said Vlad quietly. "Grandpa's asleep," he added, lifting his finger to his lips.

"We don't need to keep quiet for him," said Mortemia. "That old vampire will sleep through anything." She smiled as she took in her surroundings. "Ah, it is simply *wicked* to be back at Misery Manor. Cold and gloomy – just how I like it. None of that bright electric light that your sister has insisted on installing in Fang Towers."

"You must admit we had an EVIL time with Pavlova and Maximus," said Drax, leaning in and kissing Mortemia on the cheek.

"Tell me about your visit, Mother," said Vlad, as his father dropped into an armchair by the fire. "I want to hear all the details," he said, pretending to sound eager.

Maybe if I keep Mother talking long enough, she won't ask about the tasks she set me, he thought.

Minxie had helped him by collecting all the spiders and putting them into jars, but he wasn't sure she'd got the labelling right. And as for the flying in the dark and the Transylvanian – he hadn't managed to master those at all. At least his mind control

had progressed, although it seemed to only work on Boz. No matter how hard he had tried with Minxie, he had failed. He was dreading his mother's reaction.

Mortemia flung herself on to a chaise longue. "It was *exhausting*," she said. "All I want now is to have a good day's sleep."

Drax gave a thin smile. "Mortemia, my evil one, shouldn't you be asking our son about his week?"

"Of course," Mortemia said. "Enough of this chit-chat – I want to see if you've completed all my tasks."

Vlad groaned inwardly while Flit gave him a reassuring pat on the head with his wing.

"If I find you've been wasting time, you'll be packed off to Transylvania tonight," Mortemia added.

"I-I'll fetch the spiders," Vlad said.

Drax turned to Grandpa Gory, who was still sound asleep. He raised his voice and said, "I trust you have been keeping Vlad on track, Father?"

"What?" The old vampire woke up at the sound of his son's voice. "Ah, Drax. Hello. Yes, working all the time. And a little flying practice, of course. Not to mention some instruction in the old vampire ways, and folklore and whatnot—"

"GORY!" Mortemia roared. "I left you

144

specific instructions."

"It's all right, Mother," said Vlad, coming over with a tray full of spiders in jars. "Look."

"Show me!" Mortemia commanded.

Flit hovered over her as she picked up a jar and peered at the label.

"*Spiderus smallus?*" she shrieked. "*Spiderus fattus? Spiderus thinnus? Spiderus hairius legsus?* What nonsense is this? These are not the correct terms for these creatures!"

Vlad began trembling. "But I-I thought that… That is, I was trying to…" He felt his stomach churn – he'd had a sneaky feeling that Minxie couldn't possibly have known all the spider names! He was going to get into so much trouble now…

"What is THAT?" Mortemia snapped. She pounced at something on the floor and Vlad saw with horror that it was his book report! It must have fallen out of his cape.

Flit squealed in fear and flew up to the
rafters to hide.

Oh no. Things can't get any worse, Vlad
thought miserably.

"*The Secret Six Find Some Treasure*!" Mortemia
spat. She held the paper as though it were
the most poisonous thing she had ever seen.
"You've been writing stories about *humans*?"

"No!" Vlad cried, snatching at the paper.

But Grandpa Gory got there before him.

"Ah, that's mine," he said, taking it from Mortemia. "I was – er – doing some research. For a new book about humans – the first ever vampire history of humans and how they have … ruined our lives."

Vlad held his breath. Would Mortemia believe this?

"That does it," she hissed. "You cannot be trusted with my son, Gory, even for a few days. Bringing ideas about human life into our home! How could you?" she demanded. "Vlad must go to Transylvania to stay with Lupus tonight."

"But Mother!" Vlad protested. "I DID do the work. I collected all those spiders," he said.

Vlad was beginning to feel angry now. He'd tried so hard to do what she'd asked but nothing was ever good enough for his mother.

Vlad wished that she was small enough to be put inside a jar.

I would label her Spiderus annoyingus, he thought, closing his eyes.

He imagined a jar tipping over…

…and the spider running out…

Then he concentrated hard on an image of his mother shrinking to the size of a spider…

…and the empty jar falling over her and trapping her inside…

"AARGH! Unshrink me immediately!" came a teeny-tiny scream.

Vlad shook his head in disbelief – he'd used the power of his mind to shrink his mother to the size of a spider!

Drax was on his feet, pointing at his wife and laughing heartily.

"What fantastic work, Vlad!" cried his father. "Mwahahahahaaa! You perfect little devil, you. You take after me, I can see," he added proudly.

"Thank you, Father," said Vlad nervously. He was already dreading his mother's anger when she was turned back to her normal size.

Flit flew down and gave a batty giggle. "That's brilliant," he whispered into Vlad's ear.

"Get me out of here!" the mini Mortemia was squealing. "I am packing him off to Transylvania tonight."

"I think that's a little harsh, my devilish one," said Drax.

"Please don't send me right away, Father," said Vlad, looking up at Drax.

"In fact, I was thinking," said Drax, stroking his spiky chin. "Pavlova and Maximus were so generous to us, perhaps we should repay their hospitality and invite Lupus here first."

"Noooo!" howled the tiny Mortemia. "Vlad must be punished."

"For what?" said Drax, his face wide with innocence. "He has worked hard on his mind-control skills – he was only showing you what he had learned."

"All right, all *right*!" cried Mortemia. "Lupus will come here then, and hopefully that will shake some of the more un-vampiric things out of you, Vlad. Now, turn me back to my normal size!"

"But—" Vlad tried to protest. This was no good – he didn't want Lupus coming to stay!

Drax held up a hand to silence his son. "That's settled," he said. "I shall write to Pavlova and arrange it straight away. Come with me, my little blood vessel, I'll put you right again." And with that, he popped the

jar containing Mortemia into his pocket.

Vlad could hear his mother's muffled squeals as Drax left the room.

"Don't worry about your mother," said Grandpa Gory once Vlad's parents had gone. "At least she knows you have the power to control things with your mind now. The next thing to learn is how to make her *forget* things!" He chuckled. "When I was a young vampire, I used to do that to *my* mother all the time…"

"That's a great idea!" said Flit.

"It doesn't solve the problem of Lupus coming to stay though," said Vlad.

"I'm sure I can find ways to distract him so that you can come and have a break with me and Mulch occasionally," said Grandpa kindly.

"Is that a promise?" asked Vlad.

Grandpa smiled. "It is," he said.

"You'd better not break it," squeaked Flit,

"or you know what Vlad will do to you?"

"Yes!" said Vlad, a bubble of laughter rising up inside him. "I might just have to use mind control on you, too!"

"Oh! I can't let that happen, can I?" said Grandpa.

And they threw back their heads and laughed. "Mwhahahahaaa!"

The Secret Six Find Some Treasure!

The Secret Six met just before midnight in their camp in the woods. They had planned a special mission. They were going to go down to the beach and have a midnight feast in the cave.

"Did you bring the extra torches, Ben?" Jin asked.

"Of course," said Ben. He had headtorches for everyone. He even had a special torch for Billy's collar.

"Woof!" said Billy, wagging his tail.

"Shh!" said Charlie. "We must ALL be quiet."

"I've got the bag," said Kate.

"Don't eat the snacks before we get there!" said Prav.

Billy wagged his tail even harder. He knew about snacks!

Charlie laughed. "You'll get a treat if you're good," she said.

The Secret Six made their way carefully out of the camp, through the trees and down to the coast path. Billy found the gap in the bushes which led to the secret path. He nosed through. The children followed, pushing against branches until they came out on to the cliff edge.

"Wow!" said Prav.

The moon was full. Its silvery beam lay on the sea like a magic carpet.

The children followed Billy and Prav down the steep steps that Uncle Kevin had cut into the cliff.

"I wish we could go for a swim," said Charlie. She looked across the shining water.

"Urgh, I don't," said Kate. "There might be horrible jellyfish that come out at night."

The children arrived at the cave.

"Oh," said Prav, shivering. "It's colder in here at night."

"Let's light a fire," said Jin. "There's loads of driftwood in here from the camp we made last week." She shone her torch around, lighting up the dark floor and walls.

"What's that?" Ben exclaimed. He was pointing at a lumpy bundle, pushed back against the side of the cave.

Jin took a step towards it.

"Careful!" said Kate. "It might be alive!"

Jin called Billy to investigate. The dog ran over to the bundle, his tail wagging, his ears pricked. The light from Billy's torch fell on the bundle. The children saw that it was some kind of sack. Billy sniffed around it and then sat back on his hind legs and looked up at Jin.

"What is it, Billy?" Charlie asked, coming over. "Do you want us to have a look?"

Billy wagged his tail again. He panted excitedly, his pink tongue hanging out of his mouth.

The children all gathered around as Charlie and Jin gently pulled at the sack.

Suddenly there was a loud RIP! The sack fell open and hundreds of gold and silver coins came tumbling out.

"Oh!" gasped the children. "Treasure!"

"What are we going to do now?" Jin asked.

Anna Wilson LOVES stories. She has been a bookworm since she could first hold a book and always knew she wanted a job that involved writing or reading or both. She has written picture books, short stories, poems and young fiction series including *Nina Fairy Ballerina*, *Top of the Pups*, *The Pooch Parlour* and *Kitten Chaos*. Anna lives with her family in Bradford-on-Avon, Wiltshire.

www.annawilson.co.uk

Kathryn has a passion for illustration, design, animation, film and puppetry! She attended Sheridan College for the Bachelor of Applied Arts – 2D Animation Program and completed an internship at Pixar Animation Studios for storyboarding. She loves working on children's entertainment, publications and media – especially kids' books – and television series. She is currently based in Toronto, Canada.

www.kathryndurst.com

"SPOOKY CHARACTERS WITH
AN IMAGINATIVE STORYLINE."

SCOTSMAN

"VLAD MAY BE THE WORLD'S WORST VAMPIRE,
BUT HE'S ALSO THE MOST ADORABLE. A TREAT."

JO NADIN, AUTHOR

"A DELICIOUS STORY (EXCEPT FOR BLOOD FOR
BREAKFAST – BLEURGH!)."

ELEN CALDECOTT, AUTHOR